For my childhood dog.
—M.C.

Library of Congress Cataloging-in-Publication Data available.

ISBN 978-1-4521-7774-8

Manufactured in China.

MIX
Paper from
responsible sources
FSC
www.fsc.org
FSC™ C008047

Design by Lydia Ortiz.
Typeset in Brandon Grotesque.
The illustrations in this book were rendered in tempera and pastels.

10 9 8 7 6 5 4 3 2 1

Chronicle Books LLC
680 Second Street
San Francisco, California 94107

Chronicle Books—we see things differently.
Become part of our community at www.chroniclekids.com.

SUCH A GOOD BOY

By Marianna Coppo

x

chronicle books•san francisco

This is Buzz.

Come here, Buzz!

Good boy.

Buzz is a very lucky dog.

He lives in a very fancy house

inside an even fancier one.

He takes care of his appearance
and eats a healthy diet.

He pretty much has it all.

But, sometimes,
Buzz feels under pressure.

BUZZ I BUZZ II BUZZ III

BUZZ IV BUZZ V BUZZ ?

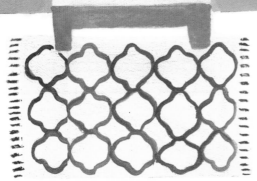

He has to keep up
the family name.

Every morning
Buzz goes for a walk.

He does his business.

He doesn't talk to strangers.

Or waste his time on nonsense.

He's such a good boy.

Buzz's favorite day of the week is Sunday.
Sunday is park day! The park is full of dogs.

But many of them
are dangerous.

Wild.

Mean.

At least that's what
he's been told.

There are others like Buzz.

You can spot them by their leashes.

Sometimes Buzz comes home with something nice.

But that never lasts long.

Sometimes
Buzz wishes he were
someone else.

It's been raining all week.

On Sunday it's sunny so Buzz can see his friends.

But, as usual, they don't have much to say to each other.

"No, no, NO!
Don't you dare, Buzz!"

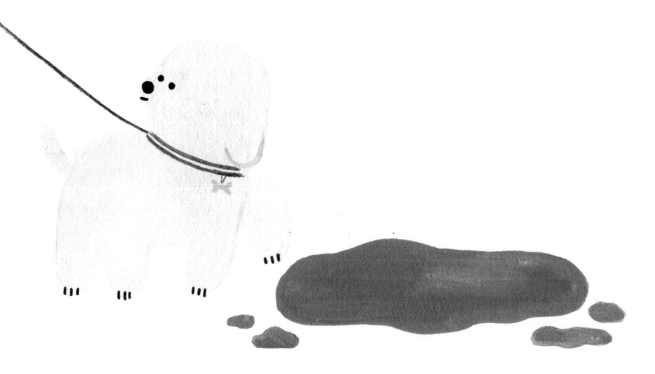

Well, he does.

GOOD BOY

15

OPEN

Maybe that wasn't
such a good idea
after all.

"Wait here. Good boy."

Good boy?

GOOD BOY PET GROOMING

15

BACK
SOON

Not anymore.

Buzz is free!

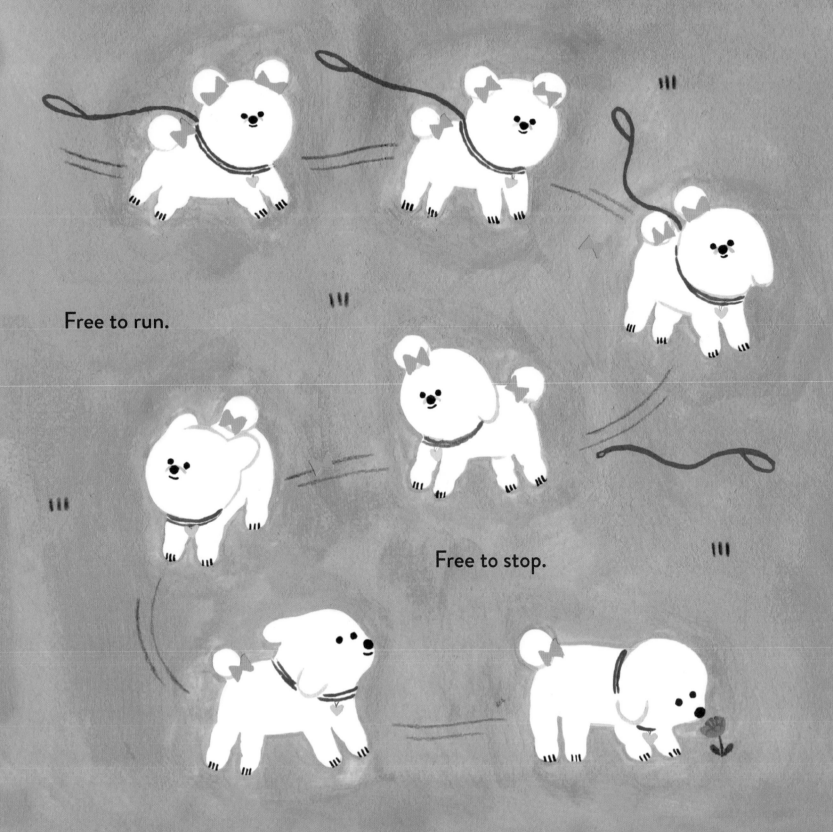

Free to run.

Free to stop.

Free to recognize   and be recognized.

Free to taste this

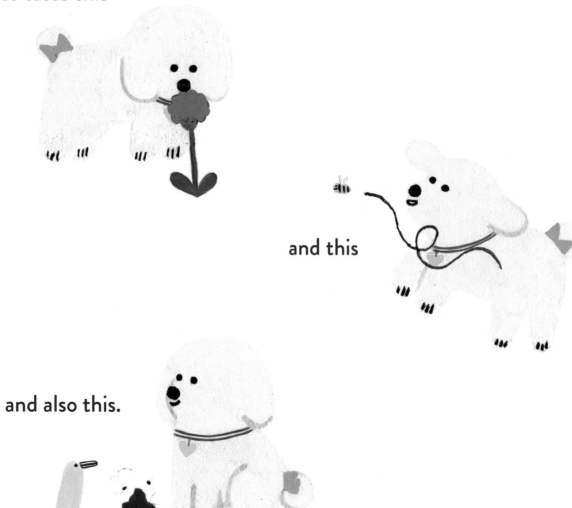

and this

and also this.

Free to dig a hole

or two

or three

or four

or . . .

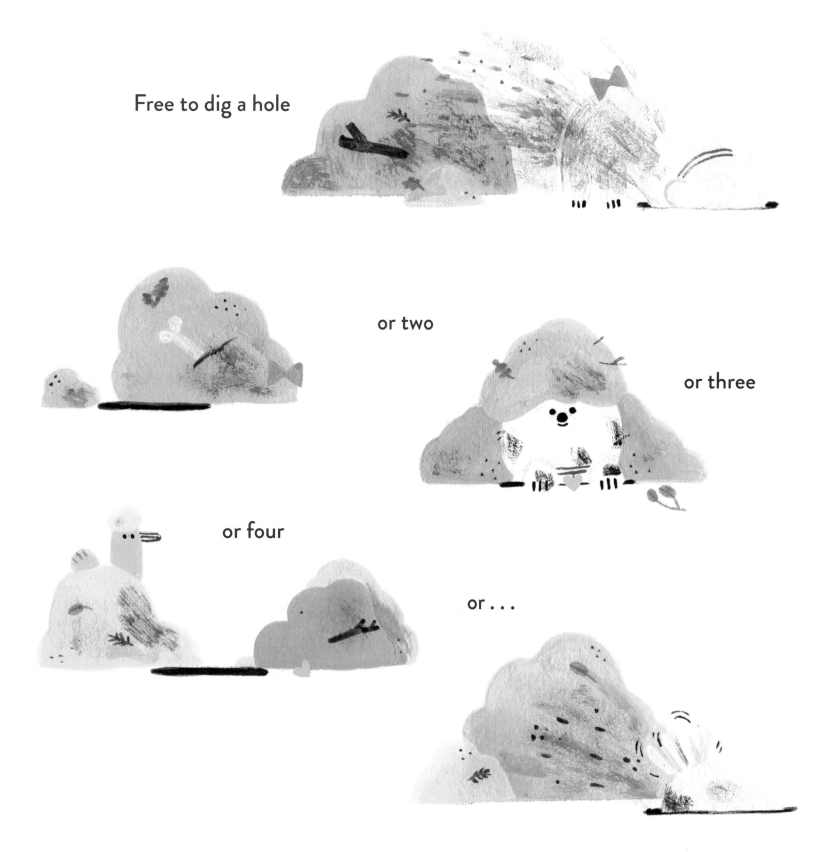

LOST
BUZZ

BIG REWARD
366 4512

LOST
BUZZ

BIG REWARD
366 4512

LOST
BUZZ

BIG REWARD
366 4512

Buzz should have known
this wouldn't last . . .

Or will it?